MEET SUPER SID, CRIME-FIGHTING KID

starring in
MEET SUPER SID,
CRIME-FIGHTING KID

BY DAN GREENBURG
ILLUSTRATIONS BY GREG SWEARINGEN

A Little Apple Paperback

SCHOLASTIC INC.
New York   Toronto   London   Auckland   Sydney
Mexico City   New Delhi   Hong Kong   Buenos Aires

ISBN 0-439-43936-1

Text copyright © 2002 by Dan Greenburg
Illustrations copyright © 2002 by Scholastic Inc.

All rights reserved. Published by Scholastic Inc.

SCHOLASTIC, LITTLE APPLE, and associated logos are trademarks and/or registered trademarks of Scholastic Inc.

12 11 10 9 8 7 6 5 4 3 2 1   2 3 4 5 6 7/0

40

Printed in the U.S.A.
First printing, December 2002

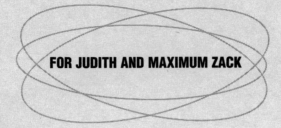

FOR JUDITH AND MAXIMUM ZACK

CHAPTER 1

It was Saturday morning and the President of the United States was phoning me from the White House. The President doesn't usually bug me on weekends.

"Sorry to bother you on a Saturday, Max," said the President, "but I have a problem. Someone or something is eating holes in the wool suits of everybody in Washington."

Oh, boy, just what I needed on a weekend

already filled with homework assignments. I was so busy, there wasn't even time to play video games. And now the President wanted me to find out why people in Washington had *holes* in their clothes?

"Begging your pardon, sir," I said, "but holes in suits just doesn't sound like that much of an emergency."

"You'd think differently if everything in your closet was so full of holes it looked like Swiss cheese," said the President. "Half the White House staff had to stay home yesterday because they had nothing to wear."

"The thing is, sir," I said, "I'm kind of jammed with homework right now. Couldn't this wait till Monday?"

"Oh, I didn't want *you* to fly down here and solve this," said the President.

"You didn't?" I said.

"No, no, of course not," said the President. "Your teacher, Mrs. Mulvahill, has complained that I'm always pulling you out of school to solve cases for me. She says I'm taking way too much time from your schoolwork. No, Max, the reason I'm calling is I want you to phone the League of Superheroes. See if they've got somebody good who can handle this thing for me. Can you do that, son?"

Hmmm. I sure didn't have time to start on another case this weekend. But get another superhero working for the President? Somehow, I didn't like that idea too much.

In case you don't know who I am, this might be a good time to fill you in.

My name is Max Silver. I'm in the sixth grade. I live in Chicago with my parents and my annoying teenage sister, Tiffany. About three years ago, I was at the Air and Space Museum in Washington and I accidentally handled some radioactive rocks that had just come back from outer space. Suddenly, I could do things most eleven-year-olds can't. Like fly. And lift trucks over my head with one hand. And run faster than a train. And cross my eyes and touch my nose with the tip of my tongue at the same time.

If I don't use my superpowers, I'm probably the second worst athlete in the sixth grade. But if I used them, I'd blow my cover and put my family in danger. You'd think I could use just a *little* of my superpowers and be just a *little* stronger and faster than other kids, but that's not how it works. With superpowers, it's all or nothing. I hate that.

Oh, I do have a few weaknesses. I'm allergic to milk, ragweed, and math. Even *hearing* a math problem makes me weak and nauseous. Superman had the same problem with kryptonite. It's pretty serious. I'm the only kid in my grade with a doctor's excuse to get out of math.

Because of my powers, the President is always sending me out on missions. Like the time an evil scientist made everything in America taste like broccoli. Or the time another evil scientist froze everybody on Earth for an hour and stole the world's greatest treasures. Or the time Iowa was invaded by evil cattle from the Planet of the Cows.

My teenage sister, Tiffany, got pretty jealous of all the attention I was getting. When her class took a trip to the Air and

Space Museum, she broke into the space rocks exhibit and handled the same rocks that gave me my powers. It gave her super-powers, too, but she never quite got the hang of how to use them.

For one thing, she never really learned how to fly. She's always bumping into birds and buildings and stuff. And she's not cool about having a secret identity. She keeps showing off and almost blowing her cover. Then I have to find something to erase the memories of anyone who guessed she was a superhero. It's a real pain. Also, she has kind of a bad attitude about being a superhero.

Anyway, back to the thing about holes in wool suits.

"Sir," I said, "I'm afraid the League of Superheroes is closed on weekends. But let me think about this a while and I'll call you back."

"Could Tiffany handle this?" asked the President.

"Uh, I'll talk to her about it, sir," I said. "Just give me ten or fifteen minutes and I'll call you back."

I hung up the phone. I didn't think Tiffany could handle this alone.

"Was that the President?" asked my mom.

"Yeah, Mom," I said. "Somebody's been eating holes in all the wool suits in Washington. The President wanted me to help him with it."

"But, Max, you've got so much homework this weekend," said Mom. "And I wanted you to do that thing for me."

"What thing?"

"Remember I showed you that awful leak in the basement? And I said maybe you could pick up the building and blow out the water with your superbreath?"

"Oh, yeah, that," I said. I don't mind helping my mom around the house, but picking up our building and blowing the water out of the basement was a lot more trouble than she thought it was.

"So somebody's been eating holes in suits?" said Mom. "Sounds like moths."

"Yeah, Mom, but this is like hundreds of suits. *Thousands* of suits."

"Then it's hundreds or thousands of moths," she said.

"Maybe," I said.

"Sounds like the President doesn't need a superhero; he needs Orkin," she said.

"Who?"

"Orkin exterminators," said Mom. "You know, the ones that advertise on TV?"

"Oh, yeah. The Orkin Man. The guy who looks like the Terminator."

"That's who he needs for this, Max. Not you."

"Yeah, well, I'm afraid I can't call the President of the United States and tell him to get an exterminator."

Tiffany came out of the bathroom. She was blowing her hair with a hair dryer.

"Was that call for me?" she shouted. I could hardly hear her over the noise of the hair dryer.

"Actually," I yelled, "it was for both of us. It was the President."

"What?" shouted Tiffany over the hair dryer.

"Turn that thing off and I'll tell you," I yelled.

She stuck her tongue out at me and turned off the hair dryer.

"I hope the President doesn't need us today," she said. "I have, like, a million things to do for school. Plus which I promised Ashley, Kimberly, and Brittany I'd go shopping with them. Plus which I just did my hair, and flying makes my hair all yucky."

"He didn't want us," I said. "He knows how busy we are. He wants me to call the League of Superheroes and get somebody else."

Tiffany looked like somebody had punched her in the stomach.

"He didn't want *us*?" she said. "After we saved, like, the whole country from those terrible creatures from the Planet of the Cows? After we saved, like, the whole world from those gross underwater people?"

I nodded. "It's not that he doesn't *want* us," I said. "It's that he knows we're busy. He asked if I'd get somebody else from the League of Superheroes."

She put her hands on her hips.

"And you're going to *do* that?" she said. "You're going to let somebody else get credit for saving the country, and not us?"

"I don't know," I said. "I might."

"What did he want us to save the country from?" she asked.

"Something is eating holes in wool suits in Washington," I said.

She rolled her eyes.

See what I mean about a bad attitude for a superhero? She doesn't like to work on cases if they sound dorky. And she cares too much about stuff like getting credit for saving people.

"Max, I think it would be, like, a really big mistake to let some other superhero do stuff for the President instead of us."

"I know," I said. "I guess you're right.

Well, then, are you willing to fly to Washington now?"

Tiffany sighed this really huge sigh. "I think our country needs us," she said.

Oh, boy. Our country didn't need us till Tiffany got worried that another superhero might get credit for solving the case. There's that attitude thing I was talking about again. What a phony she was. Although I had to admit I sort of saw her point. Does that make me a phony, too?

"What about Ashley, Kimberly, and Brittany?" I asked.

Tiffany shrugged. "I'll tell them I can't go shopping," she said.

"And what about how flying makes your hair all yucky?"

"I'll just use lots of hair spray," she said.

I turned to Mom.

"So, Mom, can we go to Washington?" I asked.

"What about all your homework?" she said. "What about picking up the building and blowing the water out of the basement?"

"Can't I do all that on Sunday?"

"I was really counting on you to do it *today*, Max," she said. "But never mind. Go to Washington."

I felt kind of guilty.

"Mom, I'm sorry," I said. "If you really want me to lift up the building today, I won't go to Washington."

"No, no," she said. "Go to Washington."

"Only if you're sure."

"I'm sure, I'm sure," she said. She sounded a little annoyed.

I picked up the phone and called the

President's private number. Somebody else answered.

"The President is on the other line," said the person. "Can he call you back?"

"No, that's OK," I said. "Just tell him that Maximum Boy and Maximum Girl are flying to the White House right away."

CHAPTER 2

The flight to Washington was OK, except that Tiffany's cape got caught on the tip of the Washington Monument and ripped. And when we tried to land on the White House lawn, she tumbled onto one of the Marine guards.

The Marines got all upset until I explained who we were. Then they started apologizing all over the place for pointing their guns at us and shouting.

"It's OK," I said. "I don't blame you for being scared when Maximum Girl landed on you."

"*Sir,* we were not scared, *sir,*" said the Marine that Tiffany fell on. "Marines are never scared, *sir*. We just did not expect a girl to fall on our heads, *sir*."

The Marines showed us to the door of the West Wing. Another guard escorted us down the hall to the Oval Office. We went inside.

"Oh, uh, hi," said the President.

He looked a little embarrassed. I thought it was because there were so many holes in his suit that you could see his underpants. But that wasn't it.

"I didn't think you guys were coming," said the President. "I thought you were too busy with homework."

I guess the President never got my message.

"Well, we *were* busy with homework, sir," I said. "But we figured our country needed us."

I didn't plan to say that; it just came out. Now I was definitely just as phony as Tiffany.

Then somebody else came into the room. It was a boy about Tiffany's age. He was wearing a superhero's outfit. A blue mask. A red cape. Red-white-and-blue tights. On his chest were the letters SSCK. He had blond hair and this really muscular body. He looked like he worked out about ninety hours a day. I hoped his voice hadn't changed yet.

"Guys, meet Super Sid, Crime-fighting Kid," said the President. "I called him when you said the League of Superheroes was closed on weekends. One of my people did some research on him. Super Sid, meet Maximum Boy and Maximum Girl."

Tiffany looked like she had just met a rock star.

"H—hi," she squeaked.

"Howya doin'?" I said.

Super Sid hadn't said a word yet, but already I hated him. Then he opened his mouth.

"Gosh," said Super Sid. "Maximum Boy and Maximum Girl. It's really an honor to meet you guys." His voice had definitely changed. Next to his, mine sounded high and stupid.

"Thanks," I said.

"I've heard so much about you," said Super Sid. "About the great stuff you did with the space cows. And the underwater people. You guys have done some fantastic work."

"Thanks," I said. I was beginning to like him a tiny bit more.

"Super Sid has done some fantastic work himself," said the President. "He cleaned up a 50,000-gallon oil spill in Alaska when a ship hit an iceberg. He saved a town in Chile from an erupting volcano. He saved a village in Africa from the Ebola virus."

"Oh, gosh, I just got lucky," said Super Sid.

"Super Sid rescued more kittens from trees last year than all the fire departments in the country combined," said the President.

"Oh, heck. Firefighters are a lot more

heroic than I am," said Super Sid. "I was just in the right place at the right time."

"Are you from Washington, Super Sid?" I asked.

"No, Cleveland," he said.

"In his secret identity in Cleveland," said the President, "Super Sid is on the baseball, basketball, and football teams of Thelma P. Flemm High School."

"H—how do you ever find the time to play all those sports and be a superhero?" squeaked Tiffany.

Super Sid smiled.

"Sports isn't the problem," he said, laughing. "I'm also editor of the Thelma P. Flemm school paper, I'm class president, and I play lead guitar in a band I started. I'm not very good on the guitar, though. I only know three chords."

"That's so cool to have your own band," said Tiffany. "What do you call yourselves?"

"The Really Nice People," said Super Sid. "Our CD should be out in about a month."

"You already have a CD?" said Tiffany.

Super Sid smiled and shrugged.

"It probably won't sell a dozen copies," he said.

"Frankly, I'm embarrassed," said the President. "If I'd thought Maximum Boy and Maximum Girl were coming, I wouldn't have called on Super Sid. Maybe you guys could all work together on this."

"Well," I said, "I don't think figuring out what's eating holes in a bunch of wool suits is going to take all three of us."

"Hey," said Super Sid. "Why don't you guys work on the holes in the wool suits?

I'll just work on the hole in the ozone layer."

I looked at Super Sid to see if he was serious. He was.

The ozone layer is a layer of gases that covers the Earth. It protects us from the harmful ultraviolet rays of the sun. Because of the way we've been polluting the air, there's now this huge hole in the ozone layer. Nobody's figured out how to fix it.

"Do you really think you can fix the hole in the ozone layer?" I asked.

"Gosh, I don't know," said Super Sid. "I'm pretty clueless about science stuff. But maybe I'll get lucky again."

"Isn't he great?" said the President.

"Oh," said Tiffany, "he's *so-o-o —* " She clapped her hand over her mouth before she said anything else. She was blushing like crazy.

Super Sid smiled at Tiffany.

"Hey, Maximum Girl," he said. "This ozone layer thing probably won't take the whole weekend. Maybe we could get a Coke or something tonight."

Tiffany was nodding her head like crazy.

"W—why don't you come to my parents' apartment in Chicago for dinner tonight?" she squeaked.

I glared at her. I couldn't believe it. She had just invited a complete stranger to our apartment for dinner! Without even asking Mom's permission. Without even thinking that she was blowing our secret identities! I just couldn't believe it!

"Uh, Maximum Girl . . ." I said. I didn't know how to explain it without making it worse.

"Gosh," said Super Sid. "That's awfully

kind of you, Maximum Girl. But I don't know how your mom would feel about a complete stranger at dinner."

"Right," I said. "And also — "

"Oh, don't worry, Super Sid," said Tiffany. "Mom is cool. She always lets me invite people to dinner without asking her first."

"That is *so* not true," I said.

"I'll call her right now," said Tiffany. She grabbed for a phone on the President's desk. "Sir, may I call my mom?" she asked.

"Be my guest," said the President.

"Maximum Girl," I said, "I really don't think that we should . . ."

But Tiffany was already talking to Mom.

"Hi, Mom, it's me," she said. "Can we invite Super Sid to dinner tonight? He's a superhero. Super Sid, Crime-fighting Kid.

He's fixing the hole in the ozone layer, and he has his own band, and they're coming out with a CD. The Really Nice People is the name of the band. Have you heard of them? Me, neither." She paused, then turned to Super Sid. "Mom says it's fine, come at six o'clock."

I covered my face with my hands. This was going to be a disaster, a real disaster.

CHAPTER 3

Tiffany gave Super Sid our address in Chicago. Then he flew off to work on the ozone layer. Tiffany and I went to look at some homes in Washington where suits had been eaten.

"I can't believe you did that," I said to Tiffany when we were alone.

"You can't believe I did what?" Tiffany asked.

"Invited a total stranger to our apartment."

"Super Sid isn't a *total* stranger," she said. "We, like, met him at the White House. He's, like, a friend of the President."

"He is *not* a friend of the President," I said. "The President only met him today, same as us. Just because you've fallen in love with Super Sid is no reason to blow our cover."

"Fallen in *love* with him?" she said. "Max, I did not fall in *love* with him."

"You did so."

"I did *not.*"

"Did so."

"Max, you are so terribly . . . *young,*" she said. "I don't even like him in that way. I just think he's nice. And I thought Mom and Dad would like to meet him, too. You know how

Mom and Dad always complain that we don't invite any of our superhero friends over."

"Mom and Dad *never* complain that we don't invite any of our superhero friends over!" I said.

"OK, well, maybe they don't," she said. "But I just *know* they're going to love Super Sid."

Tiffany and I went door-to-door in Washington, looking for clues about who or what was eating all those suits. We visited around twenty homes in the Georgetown area of Washington.

Most of the people who answered the door must have recognized us from the TV news, because they were pretty polite. They let us come into their homes. They showed us wool suits with huge holes chewed right through them, but we couldn't tell anything about who or what had done it. Some of the people who came to the door didn't recognize us and thought we were trick-or-treating out of season. They gave us candy. Which we ate.

At the forty-seventh home we visited, we got a big surprise. The lady who opened the door led us up to the attic to look at some clothes she had in storage. In the farthest corner of the darkened room crouched a burglar. Not just an ordinary burglar, either. A big, scary-looking burglar with glowing red eyes!

He had long feelers sticking out of his forehead. He was chewing on a wool pant leg, and he was almost done eating it. Just the cuff was sticking out of his mouth.

The lady who owned the house took one look at him, screamed, and fainted.

Tiffany screamed.

I screamed.

The burglar screamed, too. Then he jumped up, hitting his head on the attic ceiling. He must have been at least seven feet tall. But the weirdest thing about him was the wings. He had these enormous wings, like the wings of a moth. When he screamed, he spread his wings and they were even bigger than he was. They were all different shades of brown and tan, and they had this powdery stuff all over them, like a moth.

I was pretty freaked out. If I were an ordinary kid, I would have run away and hid. But I'm a superhero, so I figured I'd better do something superheroic. I took a running charge and head-butted him in the gut.

"Ooooffff!" he said.

Then he tried to bite me. When he

opened his mouth, you could see these really sharp teeth.

I ducked, and he missed me. I punched him in the mouth, skinning my knuckles on his front teeth. Tiffany threw a rocking chair at his head.

He began this high-pitched shrieking noise.

"Oh, you didn't like that, did you?" said Tiffany. "Max, throw more stuff!"

I looked around for more stuff to throw at him. The attic was filled with stuff. I threw a pair of skis at him. Tiffany threw a Hula hoop, which got caught around his neck. I threw a picnic cooler, a charcoal broiler, and a beach ball.

Tiffany tried to get him trapped in a volleyball net, which kind of worked. He got his feelers and one of his wings caught in the net and couldn't get free. He fell down with the Hula hoop around his neck. We both jumped on top of him, punching and kicking.

"Ouch!" he yelled. "That hurts!"

I thought I better say something official.

"You're under arrest!" I shouted.

"For what?" he said.

"For, like, eating suits and stuff," I said.

"Oh, yeah?" he said. "Since when is eating suits a crime?"

He had us there.

"You're also under arrest for breaking and entering," I said. "Breaking and entering is *definitely* a crime. Ask anybody."

"I didn't break and I didn't enter," he said.

"Then how did you get in?" said Tiffany.

"The, uh, lady who lives here let me in."

"Oh, right," I said. "Like she's going to

let a guy with glowing red eyes and huge moth wings into her home."

"If you don't believe me, ask her," he said.

We looked at the lady who owned the house. She was still out cold.

"This lady was so freaked out when she saw you, she fainted," I said.

Suddenly, the moth guy lunged at me. I wasn't expecting it, and he knocked me off balance. Tiffany grabbed his leg, but he wiggled free. Then he tore the volleyball net off him and hurled himself at the attic wall. He must have hit it pretty hard, because he tore a huge hole in the wall. Then he climbed through the hole.

"Hey, come back here!" I shouted. "I'm not done arresting you!"

The moth guy carefully pulled his wings

through the hole. Then he jumped. Tiffany and I watched through the hole. Before he hit the ground, he flapped his enormous moth wings and began to fly. His wingspan was at least fifteen feet. I had never seen anything like him before.

"He's getting away!" Tiffany screamed. "Come on!"

The lady who owned the house was just waking up. She sat up and rubbed her eyes.

"W—where am I?" she asked.

"You're in your attic," I said. "And we're leaving to catch the moth guy."

I crawled through the hole and jumped into space. Before I hit the ground, I was flying, too. My silver cape trailed after me in the wind. Tiffany was right behind me.

I could see the moth guy far ahead of us. He was swooping low over the roofs of houses, dodging the chimneys. I wondered why he was flying so low. Was it to lose us, or was it because he couldn't fly any higher with those huge floppy wings of his?

We were gaining on him. Both Tiffany and I can fly as fast as the space shuttle. Faster, even. This guy was flying only as fast as a moth. Soon we were right above him. Tiffany was on his right, I was on his left.

"Pull over!" I shouted down to him. "You're under arrest!"

He just laughed at us. I signaled to Tiffany. We both swooped down and tried to grab him. He whapped us with his enormous wings and kept on flying.

Because of those huge floppy wings, it was really hard to get to him from above. I signaled Tiffany again. We dove down and tried to grab him from underneath. But he was flying too low. There was almost no space between him and the rooftops.

We trailed after him that way for several miles. He led us to Capitol Hill. Over the Supreme Court building. Over the Air and Space Museum. Over the Smithsonian Institute. Tiffany didn't see the Washington Monument coming at her till it was too late.

"Tiffany!" I shouted. She bounced off the Washington Monument and fell with a loud splash into the Reflecting Pool.

I could either follow the moth guy or help Tiffany. I swooped down to help Tiffany. The moth guy flapped away.

"So long, suckers!" he called as he flapped.

I fished Tiffany out of the Reflecting Pool. Luckily, she wasn't hurt too badly. She

was soaking wet and she had a bump on her head the size of a Ping-Pong ball. Outside of that, she seemed fine. I couldn't understand why she was so upset.

"I cannot believe what I just did!" she cried. "How could I have been so stupid?! This is the worst day of my life! The absolute worst!"

"You mean because you smacked into the Washington Monument and the moth guy got away?" I said.

"No, Max," she said. "Because I smacked into the Washington Monument and got a bump on my head the size of a basketball, and now Super Sid will think I'm *ugly*."

We flew back home to Chicago.

CHAPTER 4

When we got home, Dad was finishing up his artwork for the day. Dad's an artist, and he's really good. He was wearing his painter's shirt, with dabs of paint all over it, and cleaning his brushes with turpentine. It smelled pretty strong.

He took us into the kitchen, where Mom was steaming some vegetables. He put peroxide on our cuts and ice on Tiffany's forehead. Her swelling started going down right away.

"So, how was Washington?" asked Dad. "Did you find out who's been eating all those wool suits?"

"Yeah," I said. "But he got away. And Tiffany fell in love."

"I did *not* fall in love!" said Tiffany.

"Did so," I said. "His name is Super Sid, and Tiffany wants to marry him. She calls him her future husband."

"Dad, Max is a dork!" said Tiffany. "Make him stop."

"If I'm a dork," I said, "then you're a super-dork."

"If I'm a super-dork, then you're a super butt-head," said Tiffany.

"Well, this is a nice mature conversation between superheroes," said Dad.

"Sorry, Dad," I said.

"Sorry, Dad," said Tiffany.

"Now tell me, Tiffany, who is this Super Sid?" Mom asked. "And why on earth did you invite him to dinner?"

"Because he's nice," said Tiffany. "I think you and Dad will really like him."

"How are we going to have dinner with him without blowing our secret identities?" I asked.

"I don't know," said Tiffany. "If you're that worried, we can both wear our costumes and masks when he's here. Even though they itch."

"But you already gave him our address and our last name," I said. "What's left of our secret identities that's still secret?"

"So, big deal," said Tiffany. "If he's a superhero, we can trust him."

"Yeah," I said. "*If* he's a superhero."

"What's *that* supposed to mean?" said Tiffany.

"Whatever you think it means," I said.

"We're having steaks for dinner," said Mom. "I hope you realize that inviting an extra person means we don't have enough now."

"Oh, Mom, I'm sorry," said Tiffany. "Don't worry. I'm a superhero. I'll figure out some way to make it work." Tiffany thought a minute. "OK," she said, "I've solved it. Super Sid can have *Max*'s steak."

"Thanks a lot, butt-cheek face," I said.

"You're welcome, underpants breath," said Tiffany.

"Children!" said Dad.

"Sorry, Dad," I said.

"Sorry, Dad," said Tiffany.

"What time is Super Sid coming?" Mom asked.

"You said to tell him six o'clock," said Tiffany.

"Well then, set the table," said Mom.

While we set the table, we watched the news on TV. There was more news on the moth guy. Clothing departments of stores in New York and Cleveland were now reporting that they had all their wool suits chewed to pieces.

A security guard in one of the Cleveland stores walked into the men's section just before the store opened. He saw a guy just like the one we fought with in Washington. He was about seven feet tall and he had glowing red eyes and huge mothlike wings, just like our guy. He escaped before the guard could stop him. Reporters were now calling him Moth Man.

At six o'clock sharp the doorbell rang. In came Super Sid. He was carrying two bunches of tulips. He gave one bunch to Mom, the other to Tiffany.

"Oh, Super Sid," said Mom. "These tulips are so fresh. Where did you get them?"

"I stopped off in Holland," said Super Sid.

"You went all the way to *Europe* to buy us flowers?" said Mom.

"Well, I had a strong tailwind," said Super Sid, "so it didn't take much time at all."

Now Mom and Tiffany were both in love with Super Sid.

"I hope you don't like steak, Super Sid," I said. *"Because we don't have enough for five people."*

"Max . . ." said Dad. He glared at me and shook his head.

"Actually," said Super Sid, "that's great, because I'm kind of a vegetarian."

"Oh, my," said Mom. "I'm so sorry. There

isn't much you can eat here then, except for some carrots and peas."

"Gosh," said Super Sid, "carrots and peas are my favorite food. But I've got a better idea. Why don't you let me take you all to dinner in Paris? It'll be my treat."

"Paris, France?" said Mom.

"Sure," said Super Sid. "Tomorrow's Sunday, so it's not a school night. If we leave now, we can have dinner at the top of the Eiffel Tower and fly back before my ten o'clock bedtime."

His ten o'clock bedtime! I couldn't believe any fifteen-year-old went to bed at ten o'clock on a weekend. He was clearly just trying to impress my parents.

"How in the world would we get to Paris?" asked Dad.

"Well, three of us fly," said Super Sid.

"I'll carry you and your wife, Mr. Silver. Maximum Boy and Maximum Girl can follow behind us. What do you say?"

Mom and Dad looked at each other. I was praying they'd say no.

"Why, I think that would be lovely," said Mom. "We've never been to Paris."

"But we certainly won't let you pay for dinner, Super Sid," said Dad.

"Oh, don't worry," said Super Sid. "It won't cost me a penny. I once saved the life of the chef at the Eiffel Tower. He never lets me pay for anything."

Mom and Dad got all dressed up. I've never seen them so excited. I've been to Paris on superhero business, so, big deal. The last time was when a supervillain stole the famous Mona Lisa painting. I wasn't in the mood to go to Paris with Super Sid tonight, but we went anyway. That's how much anybody in my family cares what *I* want.

We got to Paris in about forty minutes. Super Sid showed us all the sights. The Louvre. The Arc de Triomphe. Notre Dame cathedral. The River Seine. Mom, Dad, and Tiffany were all over Super Sid like mozzarella cheese on a pizza. They hardly knew I was there.

I saved a puppy who was drowning in the River Seine. I jumped into the water, swam out to the puppy, and then carried him back to shore. The water was cold and some of it went up my nose. The little girl who owned the puppy was so grateful, she couldn't stop thanking me. At least I *think* she was thanking me. Since I don't speak any French, I couldn't tell. When I caught up

again with Mom, Dad, Tiffany, and Super Sid, they didn't even know I'd been gone. My Maximum Boy uniform and cape were so wet I left a puddle wherever I walked, but nobody even noticed.

We went to the top of the Eiffel Tower for dinner. The view was pretty amazing, I have to admit. The setting sun made the sky fiery orange, then pink, then deep purple. The twinkling lights of Paris below us looked like thousands of lightning bugs. If I hadn't been soaking wet and in such a lousy mood, I probably would have enjoyed it.

"This is the most romantic night of my whole entire life," said Tiffany.

"Mine, too," said Mom.

"I'm getting lots of ideas for paintings," said Dad. He was drawing sketches in a little sketchbook he'd brought. "Super Sid, we really have to thank you for this."

Any second now I expected them to start hugging and kissing him. They didn't, though.

We flew back across the Atlantic Ocean and got to Chicago by nine forty-five. And then both Mom and Tiffany hugged Super Sid good night. Dad didn't hug Super Sid; he shook hands with him. *Then* he hugged him. I just shook hands with him. I was boiling inside, but I didn't know why. Then Super Sid flew home to Cleveland to go beddy-bye.

"Well, that was the best night of my life," said Dad.

"Mine, too," said Mom. "Nothing else even comes close."

"Didn't I tell you Super Sid was amazing?" said Tiffany.

"You were right," said Mom. "He's the most amazing boy I've ever met."

"Max, you seem kind of quiet tonight," said Dad. "Did you have a good time in Paris?"

"No," I said. "And my hamburger tasted like monkey puke."

CHAPTER 5

"You went *where* Saturday night?" asked Charlie Sparks.

It was about noon on Monday and we were in the school cafeteria, eating brown slop. Our school cafeteria specializes in brown slop. Sometimes they have other things. Sometimes they have *gray* slop.

"I told you, Charlie," I said. "After Tiffany smacked into the Washington Monument and Moth Man escaped, Super Sid took us to dinner in Paris."

Charlie Sparks is my best friend. She's a girl. She's the only kid who knows I'm Maximum Boy, because she's the only one I trust. You could pull out her fingernails one by one and she wouldn't ever tell you my secrets.

Charlie couldn't believe we'd gone to Paris for dinner.

"That's the coolest thing I've ever heard in my entire life," she said. "I wish I were you, Max."

"No, you don't," I said. "If you were me, you'd have to have Tiffany as a sister. And then you'd have to listen to her say all this gooshy stuff about Super Sid. I wish she'd just marry him already and be done with it."

"Hey, Max," said Charlie. "I think you're jealous."

"Jealous?" I said. "Of Super Sid? Get out of here."

"No, Max, honest," said Charlie. "You are."

I thought it over. I ate some more brown slop. I sighed.

"OK, maybe I am a little jealous," I said. "It's just that Super Sid is so great at everything. He's not only a superhero, he's a real athlete. He's on his high school team in baseball. And basketball. And football. He's got these huge muscles. He's editor of his school paper. He has his own rock band. He's got his own CD. I mean, he's perfect. Next to him, I look like a dork. A skinny dork."

"Max, cut it out," said Charlie. She

hates when I run myself down. "You're great, too," she said. "You'd be great even if you *weren't* a superhero."

"You know the worst part about Super Sid?" I said. "The worst part is that he's so modest. So humble. If you talk about his band, he says he's not a good guitar player. He says he only knows three chords. If you talk about his saving towns from erupting volcanoes or the Ebola virus, he says he just got lucky. He says he was just in the right place at the right time."

"He sounds disgusting," said Charlie.

"Honest, I think the President likes Super Sid more than me," I said. "I think my own *family* likes him more than me. In fact, I'm sure they do. I wouldn't be at all surprised if they adopted Super Sid and sent me to an orphanage."

"Max, that's nonsense," said Charlie.

"Is it?" I said. "You should have seen them Saturday night. They were gobbling up his stories like peanut M&M's. They were laughing their heads off at his jokes. They didn't even know I was there. During dinner I started choking on a piece of hamburger. They didn't even notice. I had to give *myself* the Heimlich maneuver."

I got up and took my tray to the trash bins. I dumped the rest of the brown slop. Then I came back to our table.

"You know what I think, Charlie?" I said. "I think Super Sid might not be what he seems."

"What do you mean?"

"I think he might be a phony. The whole thing could be an act. Maybe he's doing it all just to make me look bad."

"Look bad?" she said. "In front of who?"

"In front of my family. In front of the President. I think old Super Sid is trying to replace me."

"Who's trying to replace you, Silver?" said a voice behind me. It was Trevor Fartmeister, the school bully.

Trevor Fartmeister is so tough, nobody ever dares to make a joke about his name. He's huge. He's got a red buzz cut and half his left ear is missing. They say a kid even bigger than Trevor bit it off in a fight. At least that's what I heard. Then Trevor bit off the other kid's nose.

"I said who's trying to replace you, Silver?" Fartmeister repeated.

"Nobody," I said.

"Yeah? Well, you could be replaced by a coatrack," said Fartmeister.

"And *you* could be replaced by a human being," said Charlie. She's really small, but she's not afraid of anybody.

"Watch it, kid, or I'll stuff you in a trash can again," said Fartmeister.

"Don't threaten her, Fartmeister," I said.

"No?" said Fartmeister. "Why not? What would *you* do, penguin-face?"

"Nothing you'd like," I said.

Fartmeister burst out laughing.

"Is that right?" he said. "You're so scared of me, Silver, you're peeing in your pants."

He grabbed a glass of water off the table and poured it in my lap.

"See?" he announced. "Silver's so scared of me, he's peed in his pants!"

A kid named Joseph Monaco laughed. Then everybody laughed. That got me really mad. I had to watch myself, though. With my superpowers I could crumble him like a Ritz cracker. But that would blow my cover, and everybody would find out I was Maximum Boy. I could never let that happen.

But I was really mad at Fartmeister. And maybe because I was already mad at Super Sid, I pushed it a little too far. I brought up the forbidden subject. The one nobody at my school has ever dared to mention. His name.

"Fartmeister," I said. "What a stupid name. Where'd you ever get a name as stinky as that?"

Fartmeister stared at me in shock. Like I said, nobody had ever dared to make fun of his name before. The whole cafeteria got quiet. The kids knew something big was about to happen, and they crowded around our table. Fartmeister's face got redder and redder. His eyes were popping out of their sockets. A low growl began deep in his throat.

Uh-oh. What had I done? I thought of the kid whose nose he'd bitten off. I used my superpowers to make my nose as hard as stone. My nose and all the rest of me.

With a terrible roar, Fartmeister rushed at me. He grabbed me. He lifted me high in the air and threw me against the wall with all his might. I hit the wall so hard, I stuck to it. Then, slowly, I came unstuck and slid to the floor. Above me, there was an indentation in the wall the exact shape of my body. I was hurt, but I wasn't dead.

Charlie flung herself at Fartmeister and started beating him with her tiny fists.

Fartmeister didn't even notice her. He stood over me, breathing hard, trying to decide what to do next.

With my X-ray super-vision, I scanned Fartmeister's guts. I saw his lunch in his stomach. I saw the digestive juices dissolving it. I saw his breakfast moving through his intestines. Then I got an idea. With my laser vision, I heated up the gases in his intestines till they expanded.

With a surprised cry, Fartmeister grabbed his gut.

"What's the matter, Fartmeister?" I asked. "Got a pain in your tum-tum?"

I focused my laser vision on his intestines again. I heated the gases till they were ready to explode. Fartmeister doubled over in pain. And then I heard the loudest fart I've ever heard in my life.

Every kid in the room roared with laughter. Fartmeister looked really embarrassed. He ran out of the cafeteria. Everybody screamed with laughter till they cried.

CHAPTER 6

When I got home, I told Tiffany what I did to Fartmeister. She wasn't all that impressed. She's too old to have ever been bullied by him.

I got to thinking about my conversation with Charlie. I guess she was right. I *was* jealous of Super Sid. Well, who wouldn't be? I got to thinking about how stupid I felt compared to him. I got to thinking about whether he was deliberately trying to make me look bad. About whether he was trying to replace me at the White House.

From hanging out at the League of Superheroes, I thought I knew everybody in the superhero business. How come I'd never heard of Super Sid till now? I decided to call the one guy who might know something about him. Tortoise Man.

Tortoise Man is a friend of mine. He's gotten kind of old and kind of fat, but he's really nice. He doesn't do too much super-hero work anymore. Sometimes he works as a handyman. He lives with his wife in a van under a bridge in Washington.

I took out his business card and dialed his number. The phone rang three times. Then I heard an answering machine tape:

"This is Tortoise Man," said the voice on

the tape. "I can't come to the phone right now. But if you need help with an international evildoer or a clogged toilet, leave me a message and I'll call you back."

"Hi, Tortoise Man," I said. "It's Maximum Boy. Please call me at — "

"Max!" said Tortoise Man. "It's so good to hear from you!"

"Hey, Tortoise Man, I thought you were out," I said.

"Nah, I'm just screening my calls. I hear you're working on the Moth Man case. How's it going?"

"We almost nailed him in Washington," I said, "but he got away. I wanted to ask you about something else, though. Have you ever heard of a guy who calls himself Super Sid, Crime-fighting Kid?"

"Super Sid, Crime-fighting Kid? Yeah. I

hear he's working on the hole in the ozone layer."

"I mean before that," I said. "Do you know anything about him?"

"Nope."

"Maybe you could do me a favor, Tortoise Man."

"For you, Max? Anything."

"Super Sid goes to the Thelma P. Flemm High School in Cleveland," I said. "He's class president, he's editor of the school newspaper, and he's on the baseball, basketball, and football teams. He has a band called the Really Nice People. Find out anything else you can about him."

"I'll get right on it, Max," said Tortoise Man.

On the TV news we heard that the Moth Man had struck again. He had now eaten the suits in every department store in Chicago, except for one: Marshall Field's. I figured there was a pretty good chance Moth Man would hit Marshall Field's sometime tonight after closing. And we'd be ready for him.

Tiffany and I went to every hardware store and supermarket in our neighborhood. We bought up every box of mothballs we could find. Mothballs are these smelly white things people put in closets to keep moths away. We also bought the largest plastic bag we could get. Then we took it all to Marshall Field's.

We talked to the store manager. We told him our plan. He said as soon as the store closed, we could go to work.

We went home and had dinner. It was fish. How can anybody stand to eat fish?

Except for other fish, I mean. Mom said we could wait for Moth Man at Marshall Field's as long as we promised to be home by nine-thirty sharp.

After we speed-washed and speed-dried the dishes, we went back to Marshall Field's. We poured all the mothballs we'd bought into the huge plastic bag. Then we sealed it, airtight. I attached the plastic bag to the ceiling in the men's suit department. Then we sat down to wait.

"So how's your future husband?" I said.

Tiffany rolled her eyes.

"For your information, Max, Super Sid is not my future husband. He's just a friend."

"Really?" I said. "And has this friend called you since Paris?"

"Not that it's any of your business," she said, "but he gave me his cell phone number,

OK? So I can call him anytime I want to. Look, how long is this going to take? Because I've got, like, tons of history homework."

"I have no idea how long it's going to take," I said. "I don't even know if Moth Man is coming at all."

"I thought you said this was going to work."

"I said I *think* it's going to work. I can't *guarantee* it's going to work."

"So how long are we going to wait? Like, all night?"

"Tiffany, we haven't been waiting more than five minutes. Let's give it a little time."

"OK. Max, when we were stuffing mothballs into the plastic bag? I, like, broke a fingernail."

"So?"

"So I'd really like to go out and buy a new one."

"You mean right now? We're on a stake-out now, Tiffany. We're on a case."

"I know that. But you don't really think Moth Man is going to come for a while, if at all. Why don't I, like, slip out to Walgreens and buy the fingernail and a Kit Kat bar? Then I'll come right back and we can wait for Moth Man."

"What if he comes while you're gone?"

"Then you'll capture him. Max, don't be such a baby. You're very good at this, remember? Before I became Maximum Girl, you did all this alone."

"I know. OK, Tiffany. Go out and buy the fingernail."

"Cool."

Tiffany left to buy the fingernail. I waited. I didn't think Moth Man would show up for a long time. Mom had told us we had to be home by nine-thirty sharp. I really didn't think Moth Man would show up till after midnight. By which time I'd be in bed, asleep. It's tough being a superhero when you're in the sixth grade.

Suddenly, I heard something. At first I thought it was Tiffany coming back. Then I realized it takes longer than that to buy a fingernail and a Kit Kat bar. I ducked around the corner.

Into the men's department crept . . . Moth Man.

He looked around nervously. Not seeing anybody, he crept to a rack of suits. He took a tan sport coat off a hanger and held it up. At first I thought he might try it on. Then he lifted the sleeve to his mouth. He sniffed it, like a dog sniffing a juicy bone. Then he started chowing down on the sleeve.

When I stuck the huge plastic bag of mothballs to the ceiling before, I attached a long nylon rip cord. The string was so thin it was practically invisible. Now I reached out and pulled on it. The rip cord yanked open the big plastic bag. All the mothballs came tumbling out.

Most of the mothballs hit Moth Man. He seemed stunned. He sank to his knees. I stepped forward.

"OK, Moth Man, or whatever you call yourself," I said. "Your wool-eating days are over. You're under arrest. I'm taking you in."

He looked at me. He seemed kind of woozy from all the mothballs. He slumped to the floor.

"Y—you're the kid from Washington," he said.

"Right," I said. "And this time you're not getting away."

"W—who are you?"

"They call me Maximum Boy," I said.

"Maximum Boy," he repeated.

He reached weakly into his pocket and pulled out a crumpled envelope. He handed it to me. On the outside of the envelope it said MAXIMUM BOY.

"What the heck is this?" I asked. I opened the crumpled envelope. I took out the crumpled letter inside. There was writing on it that I could barely make out. I smoothed out the letter and started reading it aloud:

"DEAR MAXIMUM BOY: IF THEY WORK TOGETHER, WANDA AND JIM CAN RAKE A YARD IN FOUR HOURS. WORKING ALONE, IT TAKES JIM

TWO HOURS MORE THAN IT TAKES WANDA. HOW LONG WOULD IT TAKE EACH OF THEM TO RAKE THE YARD ALONE?"

Oh, no — a math problem! *Yaaarggh!*

I got so dizzy I couldn't stand up. I felt like throwing up. I sank to the floor.

It was a trick! I'd been tricked by a stupid, suit-eating, giant moth! What a jerk I was!

"So, Maximum Boy, we meet again!" said a familiar voice behind me.

With my last bit of strength, I turned to see who'd spoken.

It was my old archenemy, Dr. Cubic Zirkon, and his henchman, Nobblock!

CHAPTER 7

"Dr. Zirkon," I gasped weakly. "The evil scientist who . . . turned into a duck-billed platypus . . . when an experiment he was doing . . . went terribly wrong. . . ."

Dr. Zirkon cackled with delight.

"It has been too long, Maximum Boy," he said. "Much too long. When was the last time we saw you? Ah, yes, now I recall. It was underwater. We were entertaining a giant octopus and you left us. How rude of you to go without even saying good-bye."

Now I got it. The whole Moth Man thing — eating wool suits in three cities — it was just one big scheme to lure me into a trap. Well, it had sure worked.

"What are you planning to do to me, you villain?" I asked.

"Just wait and see, Maximum Boy," Zirkon cackled. "Just wait and see. Nobblock! Tie him up!"

Nobblock hit me with something hard, and I passed out.

When I woke up, it took me a minute to figure out where I was.

It seemed to be some kind of hospital operating room. I was lying down. Blinding bright lights were shining in my eyes. I could barely see. There was a funny hospital smell in the room. I had a terrible headache, and there was a taste in my mouth like I'd been sucking on pennies. I felt dizzy and I wanted to throw up.

I had to find a toilet before I threw up all over the place. I tried to get up. I couldn't. Why couldn't I get up? Then I knew. I was strapped to some kind of a table.

Wait a minute — I'm Maximum Boy. Why couldn't I break through the straps that were holding me on the table? And then I heard it. In the background a tape was playing:

"ON HER FIRST THREE MATH TESTS, ANNE RECEIVED SCORES OF NINETY-THREE, SEVENTY-NINE, AND FIFTY-EIGHT. WHAT SCORE DOES ANNE NEED ON HER NEXT TEST TO HAVE AT LEAST AN EIGHTY AVERAGE?"

Oh, no! More math problems!

On a table next to me, something else was strapped down. I squinted in the blinding light to see what it was. It was a bird — a big bird from the Galápagos Islands. I recognized it because we had studied it in science class. It was called a blue-footed booby, probably because it has bright blue feet. The blue-footed booby didn't seem any happier about being here than I was.

The door to the operating room creaked open. In waddled Dr. Zirkon, followed by his giant red-bearded henchman, Nobblock. Nobblock was carrying a gas-powered chain saw.

"So, Maximum Boy," said Dr. Zirkon. "At last it is time for our little experiment. It is the same experiment that turned me into what you see today, a duck-billed platypus.

But this time, my fine young superhero, I shall exchange your brain with that of the blue-footed booby."

"Why are you doing this?" I asked.

"For science," said Dr. Zirkon. "For science and for revenge, of course."

"Revenge?"

"To repay you for ruining my plans to steal Manhattan," he said.

"I see," I said.

That was one of my first cases for the President, the stealing of New York City. Dr. Zirkon and Nobblock had chopped the island of Manhattan away from all its bridges and tunnels. They had stuck a huge motor on one end of the island and had chugged it out to sea. Then they had demanded a trillion dollars in ransom to get it back.

I got Manhattan back all right, but only

after a terrible underwater fight. A fight in which I thought Zirkon and Nobblock got eaten by a giant octopus. A fight in which I got a lot of water up my nose. If Zirkon and Nobblock *had* been eaten by a giant octopus, I wouldn't be here now. Strapped to a table. About to have my brain taken out of my skull and put into the head of a blue-footed booby.

As long as the tape recorder played math problems, I was helpless. Unless I could think of something fast, this looked like the end for Maximum Boy. I felt sorry for my poor mom and dad. They'd miss me a lot. I felt sorry for Tiffany. Even though she'd be the last to admit it, I thought she'd miss me, too. I hoped she'd carry on the fight to triumph over injustice and evil. I felt sorry for the blue-footed booby. I hoped my brain would do it more good than it had done me.

"Do whatever you want to me, Dr. Zirkon," I said. "But let the booby go."

Dr. Zirkon burst into laughter. Crazy, honking, quacking, duck-billed-platypus laughter. It was an eerie sound.

"I shall not let the booby go," said Dr. Zirkon. "And I shall not let *you* go, either. I have spent far too much time planning this experiment to let anyone go now."

He took out a surgeon's knife and sharpened the blade. Then he waddled over to my table. He was cackling with laughter.

"Do you expect me to beg for my life?" I asked.

"*No*, Maximum Boy," said Dr. Zirkon. "I expect you to become a boy with a booby brain!" He cackled with laughter again.

Somebody came into the room. Somebody huge. I squinted in the blinding light to see who it was. It was Moth Man.

"How does Moth Man figure in all this?" I asked.

Dr. Zirkon burst into more crazy, honking, quacking, duck-billed-platypus laughter.

"Moth Man is one of my more successful experiments," said Zirkon when he managed to stop laughing. "Poor devil. Once he was an ordinary human being, with ordinary human tastes. Now he can't stand to eat anything but wool. It amused me to have him eat up all those suits. You weren't supposed to run into him in Washington, by the way — that was a mistake. Thank heavens he escaped and was able to perform his most important job: luring you to the Marshall Field's men's department and giving you that math problem."

Dr. Zirkon pulled a feather out of the booby's head and touched it with the surgeon's knife. The feather split in half, and both pieces spiraled slowly to the floor.

"So, Maximum Boy," said Dr. Zirkon, "before I make you a birdbrain, why don't you tell me your secret identity?"

"Forget about it, duck-bill," I said.

"Then I shall just remove that stupid mask of yours and see for myself," he said.

Zirkon bent over me. He reached for my mask.

Just as he touched my mask, the wall behind him exploded! Into the room burst two familiar figures — Maximum Girl and Super Sid!

"Moth Man, attack Maximum Girl!" shouted Dr. Zirkon.

Moth Man flew at Tiffany. I gasped. I was scared she couldn't handle him.

Tiffany punched Moth Man in the feelers. He seemed to lose all sense of direction. He went whirling around the room. Then he flew straight into the blinding bright lights. He screamed and fell to the floor with his legs twitching.

"Way to go, Maximum Girl!" I shouted.

"Nobblock, you fool!" screamed Dr. Zirkon. "What are you waiting for? Start up that chain saw!"

Nobblock yanked the starter cord on the chain saw. It came alive with a puff of smoke and a terrible racket in the small room.

Nobblock tried to attack Super Sid with the chain saw.

"Watch out, Super Sid!" yelled Tiffany.

"No problem," said Super Sid.

Super Sid tore the chain saw out of Nobblock's hands and hit the OFF button. He ripped the chain off the saw. Then he used it to tie Nobblock's hands behind his back.

Zirkon lunged at Tiffany with the surgeon's knife.

"Don't let him touch you with that knife!" I called to Tiffany. "It's so sharp it splits feathers in half!"

Tiffany punched Dr. Zirkon in the beak.

He screamed and collapsed. The surgeon's knife skidded across the floor. Nobblock, Zirkon, and Moth Man lay on the ground unconscious.

In the background I could still hear the tape machine: "DON IS THREE YEARS OLDER THAN MICKEY. IN TWO YEARS DON WILL BE TWICE AS OLD AS MICKEY WAS FIVE YEARS AGO. HOW OLD IS DON?"

"Max, are you all right?" asked Tiffany.

"No," I said. "But I will be as soon as you turn off that stupid tape recorder."

Tiffany turned off the tape recorder. The math problems stopped. *Whew!* I shook my head to shake out the dizziness. I felt my strength streaming back into my body. I broke the straps that held me to the table and stood up. Then I went and freed the blue-footed booby.

"Thanks, guys," I said to Tiffany and Super Sid. "You really saved our lives. How did you ever find me?"

"I was, like, coming back from Walgreens," said Tiffany. "I saw Zirkon and Nobblock dragging you out of Marshall Field's. I didn't know if I could take both of them without breaking another fingernail. So I followed you and called Super Sid from a pay phone."

"I immediately flew here from Cleveland," said Super Sid. "Even though it was way past my bedtime."

I was grateful to Super Sid for saving my life, but it was also pretty humiliating.

"What should we do with this poor bird?" I said. I scratched the booby behind the ears, or where I figured the ears ought to be.

"We could bring him to the zoo," said Tiffany.

"He won't be happy cooped up in any zoo," I said. "He's a native of the Galápagos Islands."

"If it weren't so late," said Super Sid, "I'd fly him down there right now."

"Why don't we take him home with us tonight?" said Tiffany. "Mom and Dad won't mind. Then we can fly him to the Galápagos tomorrow, right after school."

CHAPTER 8

"It's bad enough with you kids coming home at ten o'clock," said Mom. "But what are we going to do with such a big bird? And who painted his feet blue?"

"Nobody painted him, Mom," I said. "He's a blue-footed booby, and we're flying him to the Galápagos Islands tomorrow, right after school."

I still hadn't gotten over the humiliation

of being saved by Tiffany's boyfriend, when the phone rang.

"Who on earth would be calling us at this hour?" asked Dad. He picked up the phone. Then he said, "Just a minute, I'll get him," and handed it to me.

"Hello?" I said.

"Max, it's Tortoise Man," said Tortoise Man. "I'm sorry to be calling you so late, but I've got some important news. I thought you'd want to hear it as soon as possible."

"What is it?" I said.

"I checked out your buddy Super Sid with the Thelma P. Flemm High School."

"Really? What did you find out?"

"The president of the class is not Super Sid, Max. It's somebody named Lily Engelbert. And the editor of the school paper is somebody named Michelle Nagler. Lily is

on the chess team, and Michelle is on the recycling team."

"You're kidding me," I said.

"No, Max, I'm serious," said Tortoise Man. "And, by the way, there *is* a band in Cleveland called the Really Nice People. . . ."

"Really?"

"Yes," said Tortoise Man, "but it's made up of six elderly grandmas playing accordions. Max, Super Sid, Crime-fighting Kid, is an impostor!"

To be continued in
Maximum Boy #8:
The Worst Bully in the Entire Universe

**Check out this sneak
preview from the next
nail-biting Maximum Boy Adventure!**

The Worst Bully in the Entire Universe

Tiffany was flying on ahead of me, probably because she wanted to get this over with and be back in time to buy lipstick.

"Hey, Max, look over there!" she yelled. "There's Devil's Tower!"

"Devil's Tower is across the border in Wyoming!" I yelled. "We've gone too far!"

"Ooh, I've always wanted to see Devil's Tower!" she yelled. "That was where the

UFO came down in *Close Encounters of the Third Kind.* Can't we stop there?"

"I thought you were in a hot hurry to go home and buy lipstick!" I yelled. "The sooner we get rid of the nose-glasses on Mount Rushmore, the sooner you can go home and buy lipstick!"

"Fine!" she said in this really annoyed voice.

Tiffany made a sharp U-turn in the air and turned back toward South Dakota.

We were over Mount Rushmore in about three minutes. Even from the air we could see the funny nose-glasses. Thick-rimmed glasses with huge fat noses and bushy mustaches attached to them. The four heads on Mount Rushmore — George Washington, Abraham Lincoln, Thomas Jefferson, and Theodore Roosevelt — had taken decades to carve out of the mountain. How could anyone put up nose-glasses so fast? And then I thought – maybe the person who did this was a supervillain!

We landed on the top of Mount Rushmore and looked down on the nose-glasses. They were huge, and they seemed to be made out of some kind of gray plastic.

Tiffany and I carefully made our way down the face of George Washington and tried to see how the nose-glasses had been attached to his face.

"It looks like they are attached with Crazy Glue," said Tiffany.

"I agree," I said. "Well, Crazy Glue is pretty hard to dissolve. But not if you have laser vision. Tiffany, do you know how to turn on your laser vision?"

"Well, *duh*," she said.

"Does duh mean yes?" I asked.

Tiffany rolled her eyes. Even though she was wearing her Maximum Girl mask, I could tell.

"Yes, Max," she said. "I *do* know how to turn on my laser vision. Contrary to what you may think, I am not, like, an absolute *moron*."

"Good," I said. "I'm glad you're not an absolute moron."

Tiffany took the right side of Washington's nose, I took the left.

I turned on my own laser vision. I focused the red beam on the bridge of George Washington's nose and moved it around the outside of the nose-glasses. The laser made a nice sizzling sound as it worked. The nose-glasses came away from Washington's face.

All at once, I heard a loud popping noise

from the other side of the nose where Tiffany was working.

This was followed by a shower of sparks.

This was followed by a loud cracking noise.

This was followed by Tiffany's voice saying, "Uh-oh."

Then, all at once, George Washington's nose cracked at the base and slid completely off his face. . . .

ABOUT THE AUTHOR

When he was a kid, author Dan Greenburg used to be a lot like Maximum Boy — he lived with his parents and sister in Chicago, he was skinny, he wore glasses and braces, he was a lousy athlete, he was allergic to milk products, and he became dizzy when exposed to math problems. Unlike Maximum Boy, Dan was never able to lift locomotives or fly.

As an adult, Dan has written more than fifty books for both kids and grown-ups, which have been reprinted in twenty-three countries. His kids' books include the series The Zack Files, which is also a TV series. His grown-up books include *How to Be a Jewish Mother* and *How to Make Yourself Miserable*. Dan has written for the movies and TV, the Broadway stage, and most national magazines. He has appeared on network TV as an author and comedian. He is still trying to lift locomotives and fly.

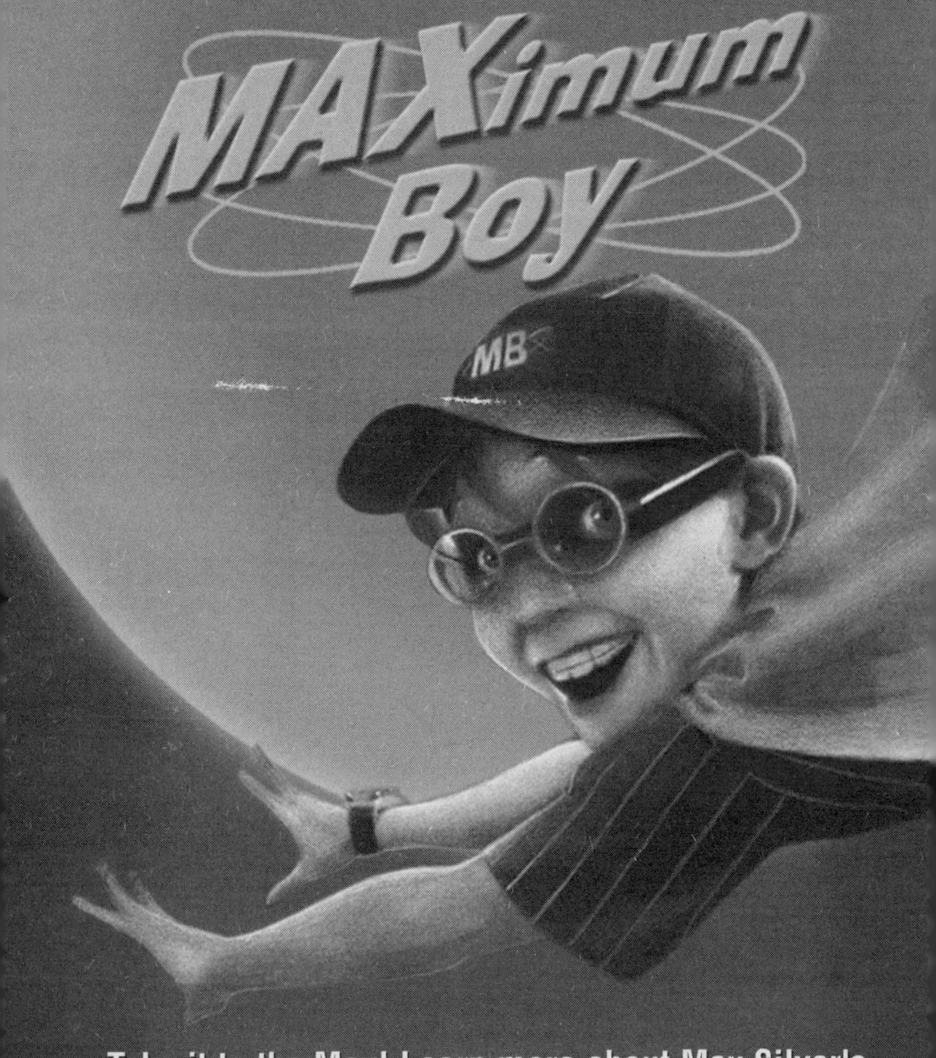
MAXimum
Boy
MB